I'm Sad Too...
And It's Okay

Written by
Georgette D. Jackson and Marcus A. Jackson

Published by Georgette Jackson
Produced by Create and Blossom
712 Austin Avenue
Waco, TX 76701
www.createandblossomstudios.com

ISBN: 978-1-945304-60-6 paperback

Printed in the United States of America

First Edition

Dedication

In memory of my beautiful mama,
Demetria (Dee) Jackson-Robinson, my best friend who
always encouraged me to express myself freely.

I'm sitting here all by myself
And that's how I want it to be
I'm thinking about never seeing my mama again
So, I don't want anyone bothering me

People are hugging each other
And my Nana hugs me too.
Then she sends me to play with the kids But
that's not what I want to do.

What happens when people die?
Tell me, where do they go?
People say they're in a better place,
But where is that? Tell me, I want to know.

SALE

A rain of tears
Falling from each eye
Can anyone help me understand
Why my mama had to die

And now we are sitting at a table
Filled with all kinds of food
People are sharing stories about my mama
But I am not in the mood!

I want my mama back
I don't want to laugh or play.
I wish she was still here
And all these people would go away.

I felt so sad
I couldn't believe this was true
That mama is gone forever
What am I going to do?

What will the other kids think
They will see that I am sad
And if one of them say the wrong thing
I'm going to get really mad!

Come sit with me Marcus
And listen to what I have to say
I know how sad you are and I am too
You have every right to be and it's okay

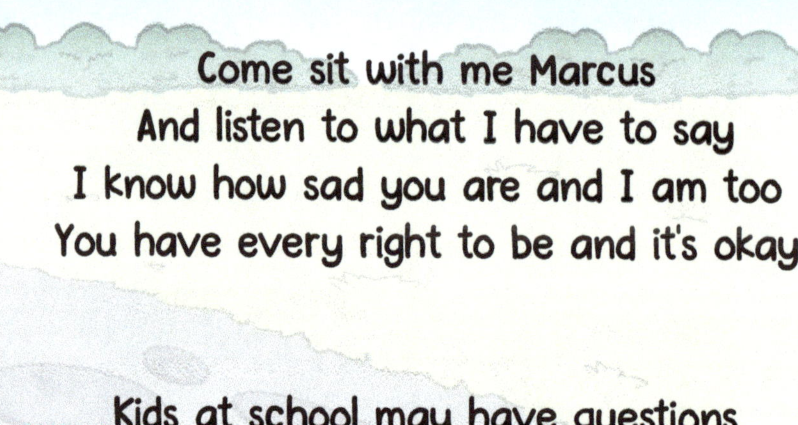

Kids at school may have questions
And ask why did your mama die
You can tell them you don't want to talk about it Or tell
them she was sick and that's the reason why

"I know how much you loved your mama
Her hugs and kisses you will miss.
I will miss her terribly too
Together, we will get through this."

When you are feeling sad
And don't know what to do
Find someone like my Nana
That you can talk to

Some days I still get sad
But I know that it's okay
My heart will slowly heal
Now it's time to go outside and play!

About the Author

Georgette is the published author of 3 books; 30 Days of Divine Rest, Heart to Heart, Inspiration in the Mourning, and her fourth book is an anthology, Champions in the Ring. Georgette is a podcast host of Get A G.R.I.P. (Grace, Restoration, Inspiration, Prayer) which speaks to the hearts of those experiencing grief. Georgette recently launched Heart 2 Heart Creatives and The Authors Room where she brings authors together to not only promote their books but to give them a platform in which to tell their "Why" behind each book. Georgette demonstrates great compassion for the homeless, the hopeless, and the brokenhearted. She has a servant's heart and is affectionately known as an encourager and inspiration to those who know her. Georgette is the founder of a nonprofit organization, Divine Rest, Inc. which assists single homeless women. She also loves to steal away to a quiet place to read, pray, and write as she hears from God. Georgette also loves to travel! Georgette has spoken on several platforms and has been featured in several magazines, podcasts, WSAV, WTOC, Atlanta Live, and several local radio stations. Georgette is available for speaking engagements as she enjoys being a willing vessel for the kingdom of God. Her motto and how she ends her podcast is "Have hope for a better tomorrow!"

Marcus A. Jackson, resides in South East GA and is gainfully employed as an Engineer Technician. Marcus has gained a love for writing poetry and shares his spoken word on social media. Marcus loves to read and study the word of God. Marcus aspires to write more books to encourage young people to explore releasing their inner thoughts and feelings onto paper.